Franklin's Neighborhood

To Auntie Trena and Uncle John — S.J.

For my neighbors in the town of Port Perry — B.C.

Franklin is a trade mark of
Kids Can Press Ltd.

Kids Can Press is a
Nelvana Company

ISBN 0-439-08369-9

Text copyright © 1999 by P.B. Creations Inc.
Illustrations copyright © 1999 by Brenda Clark Illustrator Inc.

Written by Sharon Jennings and based on the character Franklin created by Paulette Bourgeois and Brenda Clark.

Interior illustrations prepared with the assistance of Shelley Southern.

All rights reserved. Published by Scholastic Inc., 555 Broadway, New York, NY 10012, by arrangement with Kids Can Press Ltd. SCHOLASTIC and associated logos are trademarks and/or registered trademarks of Scholastic Inc.

12 11 10 9 8 7 6 5 4 3 2 1   9/9 0 1 2 3 4/0

Printed in the U.S.A.   23

First Scholastic printing, September 1999

Franklin's Neighborhood

Written by Sharon Jennings
Illustrated by Brenda Clark

SCHOLASTIC INC.
New York Toronto London Auckland Sydney
Mexico City New Delhi Hong Kong

FRANKLIN could count to ten and back again and say the alphabet without stopping. He liked drawing pictures and he loved show-and-tell. So when Mr. Owl assigned the first project of the year, Franklin was ready.

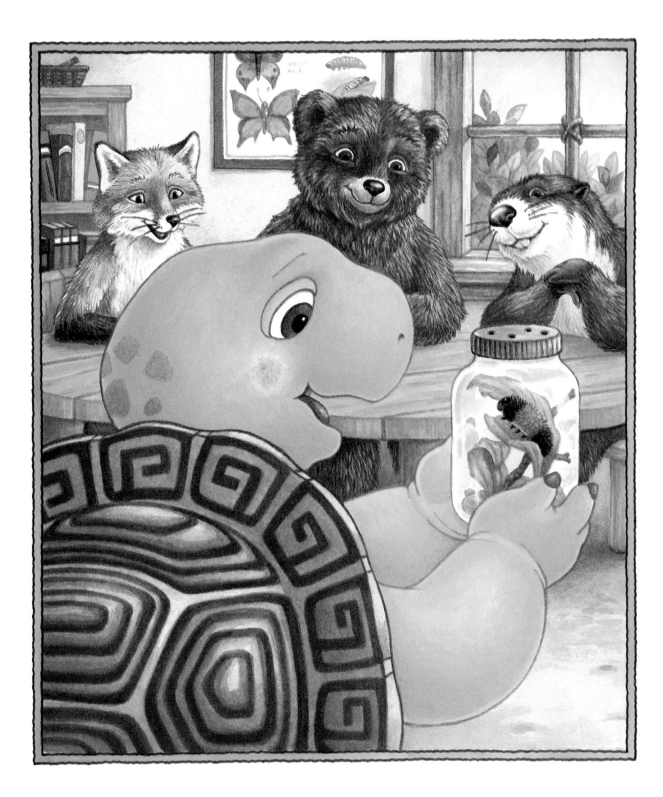

"We live in a neighborhood," explained Mr. Owl. "And our neighborhood is made up of houses and stores and —"

"Gardens," said Snail.

"And a hospital," added Badger.

"Exactly!" said Mr. Owl. "Now, for tomorrow, I want each of you to draw a picture of what you like best about our neighborhood."

"What do you like best?" asked Franklin.

Mr. Owl thought for a moment.

"The school," he replied.

Everyone laughed.

When Franklin got home, he hurried to his room.
"Do you want a snack?" asked his mother.
"No thanks," said Franklin. "I have a project to do."

Franklin took out his crayons and some paper. Then he sat down to think.

He thought about the ice cream store, then the bicycle trail, and then the soccer field.

Franklin sighed. Choosing the best thing about his neighborhood was not going to be easy.

Franklin went to find his mother.

"Could I have that snack now, please?" he asked. "I think my brain is hungry."

But after three fly cookies and two glasses of milk, Franklin still hadn't decided what he liked best.

"Why don't you go for a walk around the neighborhood?" suggested his mother.

"That might help," said Franklin. He got his paper and crayons and off he went.

Franklin met Beaver in the meadow.

"I've finished my project," Beaver announced. "I picked the library, and I went there right after school to draw my picture."

Franklin thought about storytime with Mrs. Goose, the librarian.

"That's a good idea," Franklin said. "Maybe that's what I'll draw."

He waved good-bye and headed for the library.

Franklin was sitting on the library steps when Fox came by.

"Have you finished your project?" asked Fox.

Franklin shook his head. "I was going to draw the library, but on the way here I saw the movie theater. I can't make up my mind."

"I chose the fire station," said Fox.

Franklin remembered the time Chief Wolf let him sit in the fire truck.

"That's a good idea," Franklin said. "Maybe that's what I'll draw."

He collected his paper and crayons and set off.

Franklin was outside the fire station when he saw Moose.

"Have you finished your project?" asked Moose.

"No," Franklin sighed. "I was going to draw the fire station, but on the way here I saw other places I like just as much."

"I like the pond best of all," said Moose.

Franklin thought about swimming and skating with his friends.

"That's a good idea," Franklin answered. "Maybe that's what I'll draw."

He said good-bye and headed for the pond.

Franklin was staring at the water when Bear came along.

"What's the matter?" asked Bear.

"I can't decide what to draw for my project," said Franklin. "I like too many things."

"My best place is the berry patch," said Bear.

Franklin thought about all the times he and Bear had picked berries together.

"See?" said Franklin. "Another great idea!"

"What about the park?" Bear suggested.

Franklin thought about playing with his friends on the swings and slide.

"That's it!" declared Franklin.

He said good-bye to Bear and hurried off.

Franklin's mother found him sitting alone on the teeter-totter.

"Did the walk help?" she asked.

"Not really," replied Franklin. "There are so many great things in our neighborhood."

Franklin's mother gave him a hug.

"Let's go home and talk," she said. "I made your favorite supper."

Franklin grinned. "At least I know what *that* is!"

Franklin felt a little better after broccoli soup and fly pie.

"I'm ready to think again," he said. Then he asked his parents what they liked best about the neighborhood.

"I like the farmers market on Saturday mornings," said his mother.

Franklin smiled. He loved Farmer Rabbit's sweet peas and Farmer Squirrel's fly brownies.

"And I like belonging to my chess club," said his father.

Franklin agreed. He liked belonging to the chess club, too.

Then Franklin remembered something.

"Is it true that Mr. Heron is moving?" he asked. Mr. Heron was the president of the chess club.

"Yes, it is true," replied Franklin's father. "I'm going to miss him very much. This neighborhood won't be the same without him."

Franklin nodded. He was going to miss Mr. Heron, too.

Suddenly Franklin knew what he wanted to draw.

"I know what I like best!" he said.

Franklin ran to his room and started working.

At school the next day, everyone was excited. It was time to see the projects.

Raccoon went first. "I drew the river," he said.

"I drew the forest," said Hawk.

Finally, it was Franklin's turn. He unrolled a huge sheet of paper.

It was covered with drawings of
almost everyone that Franklin knew.
"I don't get it," said Beaver.

Franklin smiled.
"I drew my neighbors," he said. "That's what
I like best about my neighborhood."